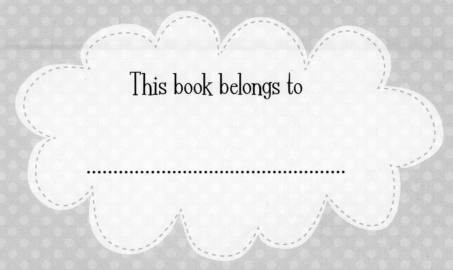

This book belongs to

....

Copyright © 2013

make believe ideas ltd

The Wilderness, Berkhamsted, Hertfordshire, HP4 2AZ, UK.
565 Royal Parkway, Nashville, TN 37214. USA.

www.makebelieveideas.com

Written by Tim Bugbird.
Illustrated by Lara Ede.
Designed by Annie Simpson and Sarah Vince.

Clara

the Cookie Fairy

Tim Bugbird · Lara Ede

make
believe
ideas

Once there were three Fairy Scouts — Clara, Kat, and Jan, who lived on a mountain in a fairy camper van.

They sold special **cookies** – a Fairy-Scout tradition – to buy the things they needed for their **camping expeditions!**

Clara's wand made cookies, tasty, crisp, and sweet,

and Kat's made **pretty** boxes
to keep them nice and **neat**.

Last of all, Jan's wand made a special fairy **bow**.
With every cookie **baked** and **boxed**, the friends were good to go!

Then, one summer's evening, they were driving out to dine,
when Clara's eye was caught by a giant roadside sign.

The sign read:

MIGHTY MEGA-WANDS

make cookies with chocolate chips!

Clara said, "I want one now! I can't let this chance slip!"

Clara picked the **biggest** wand and stood in line to pay.
Her old one looked too **boring**
so she **threw**
it right away!

Pay here

But Clara **wasn't** careful and her wand was a little **brittle.**

She **whooshed**

and **swooshed** it way too much

and it **Snapped**

right in the

middle!

The fairies tried to fix the wand
with string and tape and glue.
But not one thing would make it work.
Now what could they do?

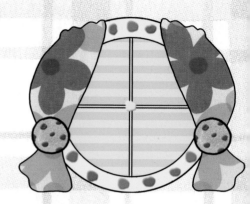

glue

craft box

Kat said, "Only **one** thing will put us back on track — we must find the **fairy garbage truck** and get your old wand **back!**"

The fairies drove across the land,
searching high and low,
'til Jan saw a junkyard
in a meadow
down
below.

"There's the **truck!**" cried Jan,
and she gave a little **cheer.**
"Let's fly down and look around.

Your **wand** just must be here!"

Unwanted wands were everywhere –
the place was overrun!
Lots looked just like Clara's,
so they tried them one by one.

The **friends** spent many hours
waving wands **around**.
But **not one** of them made cookies.
Clara's wand could not be **found**!

The fairies were getting **worried**.

Things weren't going well.

How would they fund their camping trip
if they had no cookies to sell?

Then Clara said, "Stop! Look down!"
And suddenly it was clear.
What the wands had been making

was fairy camping gear!

There were
pots and pans,
forks and spoons,
Kettles and cans,
and guitars to play tunes!

There were balls and bats,
three fairy bikes,
bright summer hats,
and boots for long hikes!

"These wands should be used,

not thrown away,"

said Clara with a frown.

"But if we put our heads together,

we can turn this right around!"

And in a flash it came to her,

a new Fairy-Scouting venture.

They'd move to the meadow

and transform the yard

into a Swap and Recycling Center!

Fairies came from **far** and **wide**
with their **wands**, unwanted or broken,
to swap or make into something new.
The center was **always** open!

And then one summer's day,
Clara had a huge surprise.
She waved the wand a fairy had found
and cookies fell from the skies!
"This is my wand!" cried Clara,
"And it works just as it should.

It's not a 'mighty
mega-wand,'
but to me it's
twice as good!"

Clara learned to care for things, and not just throw them away.

To swap or recycle, if you can, is always the better way!